Chinese Tale Series

中 国 神 话 故 事

Yu Gong Removed the Mountains

愚 公 移 山

Adapted by Cai Yunhui, Zhang Guangshuai

Translated by Liu Guangdi

Illustrated by Cai Yunhui, Zhang Guangshuai

改编　蔡云晖　张光帅

翻译　刘光第

绘画　蔡云晖　张光帅

DOLPHIN BOOKS

海 豚 出 版 社

First Edition 2005

ISBN 7-80138-567-5

© Dolphin Books, Beijing, 2005

Published by Dolphin Books
24 Baiwanzhuang Road, Beijing 100037,China

Printed in the People's Republic of China

Once upon a time, there were two big mountains in China, called Wangwu and Taihang respectively, covering an area of seven hundred square *li*, as high as tens of thousands of *zhang*.

传说中国古时候有两座大山，分别叫做王屋和太行，方圆七百里，高达几万丈。

The people living at the foot of the mountains were blocked by the mountains so it was very hard for them to go out.

　　住在山下的人们被大山阻挡了道路，出行非常不方便。

An old man called "Yu Gong" (Foolish Old Man) and his family lived north of the mountains.

有一个叫愚公的老汉，他和家人住在山的北面。

Yu Gong was more than ninety, but he was still very strong, and kept working every day.

愚公已经90多岁了，但是身体非常硬朗，每天都在劳动。

Yu Gong was very persevering in whatever he did. No matter what he did, he would go on to the end, and never stopped before reaching his goal.

　　愚公做事非常有恒心，无论做什么事，他一定要有始有终，不达目的，誓不罢休。

Owing to the blockage of the two big mountains, the family of Yu Gong had to bypass them whenever they went out, and their journey would increase by hundreds of *li* each time.

由于两座大山的阻挡，愚公一家出门都要绕道而行，每次都要多走上百里的路。

Yu Gong was always thinking how to solve the problem, and people often saw him gazing at the big mountains in deep thought.

愚公一直想要找个办法解决这个难题，人们时常能看见他望着大山凝神思索。

One day, Yu Gong looked very happy. He told anyone he met with, "I have found the way out!"

一天，愚公显得非常高兴。他逢人就说："我有法子了。"

At night, Yu Gong summoned the whole family together, and said, "Let's put our strength together to remove these two big mountains so as to open up a great road. Do you agree?" All his family said yes.

晚上，愚公把家人都召集到一起，说："让我们齐心协力搬掉这两座大山，开出一条大路，你们说行吗？"家人纷纷表示赞同。

Only Yu Gong's wife expressed some doubt, saying, "Just by such little strength you have, you cannot even remove a small hill like Kuifu, how can you get rid of the two great mountains of Taihang and Wangwu? By the way, how can we dispose of the stone and earth dug out?"

只有愚公的妻子表示怀疑，说："就凭你这点儿力气，像魁父那样的小山包，恐怕都搬不掉，又能拿太行、王屋这两座大山怎么样呢？再说，挖出来的那些石头和泥土又往哪里扔呢？"

Yu Gong kept silent. But his children said, "Move them to the side of the Bohai Sea, north of Yintu."

愚公沉默不语。他的儿孙们却说："把它们堆到渤海的边上，隐土的北面去。"

Yu Gong smiled, twisting his beard. When his wife saw everyone so determined, she stopped saying any words against it.

愚公捻着胡子露出了微笑。他的妻子看见大家都这么坚决，也就不再说什么了。

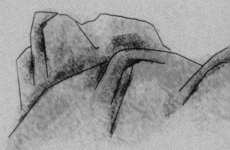

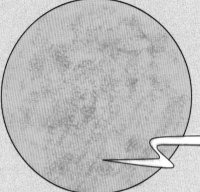

On the early morning of the next day, Yu Gong took his three sons and three grandsons to the foot of the big mountains.

　　第二天清晨，愚公就带着三个儿子、三个孙子来到了大山脚下。

They set themselves to their work, using the sledgehammers, the spades, the bamboo baskets and so on.

他们手里拿着大锤、铲子、箩筐干了起来。

The mountain stone was so hard that when the hammer hit it, sparks flew off in all directions.

山石异常坚硬，锤子砸上去，火星四溅。

However, Yu Gong and his children did not shrink back, and took turns cutting the mountains.

但是愚公和他的儿孙们并没有退却，一个个轮换着来开山凿石。

The sleeping Mountain God was awakened
by Yu Gong and his family.

沉睡的山神被愚公一家吵醒了。

Mountain God walked out of his cave, and saw a group of people knocking at the foot of the mountain.

山神从自己的洞里出来，看到一群人在山脚处敲打着。

Mountain God changed himself into an old lady
to ask Yu Gong what they were doing.

山神变成一个老太太去问愚公在做什么。

Yu Gong said that he and his descendants were
opening up a great road in Taihang and Wangwu.

愚公说他和儿孙们要在太行和王屋山
中开出一条大道。

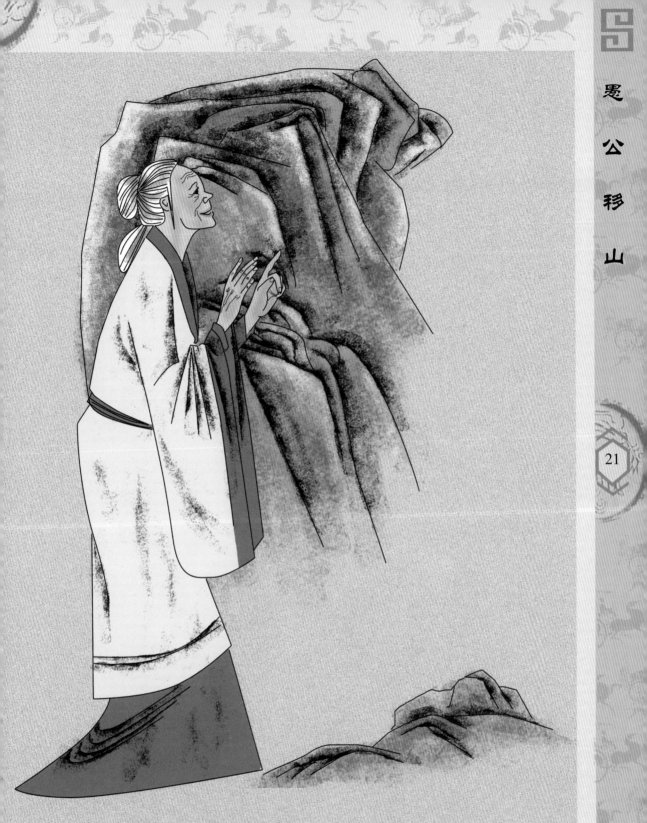

Mountain God had a good laugh after hearing it, "You see, Taihang and Wangwu Mountains are so big, what you are doing is far beyond your ability, haha!"

山神听后哈哈大笑:"这太行和王屋山这么大,你们这些人太不自量力了。"

Yu Gong and his descendants did not care about
Mountain God's mocking, and continued to
break the stone with their hammers.

愚公和他的儿孙们并没有理会山神的
嘲笑，还是一锤又一锤地砸着石头。

Led by Yu Gong, they worked night and day, carrying the heavy stone to the Bohai Sea. Thus, they shuttled back and forth between the mountains and the sea around the clock.

在愚公的带领下，他们披星戴月地挑着千斤重担将石头运到渤海边倒掉，就这样日夜不停地在山和海之间穿梭。

From winter to summer, they could take a roundtrip only once.

从冬到夏，他们才能往返一次。

Yu Gong had a neighbor, who was moved by the family's spirit. So he took his seven-year-old son to the worksite.

愚公有个邻居被他们一家的精神所感动，就领着 7 岁的儿子来到工地上。

中国神话故事

The little child also joined the mountain moving team of Yu Gong, and their enthusiasm became even greater.

小孩子也参加到愚公移山的队伍中，大家的干劲儿更足了。

The news about Yu Gong removing the
mountains spread out very soon. Many
people supported him. They came to offer
them food or water, or joined the mountain
digging work.

　　愚公移山的消息很快就传开了，
人们都很支持他，纷纷来送饭、送水、
一起挖山。

Yu Gong had a friend, called "Zhi Sou" (The Wise Old Man), the so-called cleverest man there.

　　愚公有个朋友，叫做智叟，号称是他们那里最聪明的人。

After hearing the news about Yu Gong removing the mountains, Zhi Sou hurried over to persuade him, "For such an old man as you, leading so few people, how can you remove these two great mountains?"

　　智叟得知愚公移山的消息后，急忙跑来劝他："像你这把年纪的人，带着这么少的人，怎么能移走这样大的两座山呢？"

Yu Gong laughed, saying, "Look, I have
so many children and grandchildren!"

愚公笑到:"你看看,我还有这
么多的儿孙呢?"

Zhi Sou shook his head again and again, "Impossible. It is impossible for manpower to conquer Heaven." He advised Yu Gong to give up such a foolery.

　　智叟连连摇头："不可能，人力是不可能胜天的。"他劝愚公放弃这种愚蠢的行动。

Yu Gong refuted, "I think you are too stubborn, and ignorant, even not as clever as a child! Although I will die, I have my sons! My sons can bear grandsons, and my grandsons can bear their sons... In this way, my descendants will never come

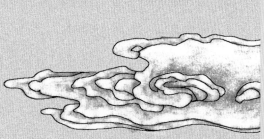

to an end! But the two mountains will never grow higher, so, Am I afraid of being unable to level them?"

愚公反驳道: "我看你太顽固了,简直不明事理,连那小孩儿都不如! 虽然我会死的,可是我还有儿子呢! 儿子又生孙子,孙子又生儿子,这样子子孙孙是不会断绝的呀! 而这两座山再也不会增高了,还怕挖不平吗?"

Zhi Sou had no word to say, and had to go disapprovingly.

智叟无言以对，只好悻悻地走开了。

Day after day, and year after year, Mount Taihang and Mount Wangwu became smaller and smaller because of their work.

日复一日，年复一年，太行和王屋山越挖越小了。

Mountain God was frightened, and when he ran up to the peak to have a look, he saw Yu Gong, his children and some local people digging very enthusiastically.

这可把山神吓坏了，他跑到山顶一看，愚公和他的儿孙、乡亲们正挖得起劲儿。

Mountain God muttered, "If they work on like this, sooner or later, the two big mountains will be leveled. Then, where should I go to live?"

山神嘀咕："要是照这样挖下去，两座大山迟早要挖没的，到时我该到哪儿去住呢？"

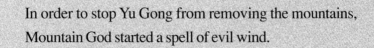

In order to stop Yu Gong from removing the mountains, Mountain God started a spell of evil wind.

为了阻止愚公移山，山神吹起了一阵妖风。

Immediately, a heavy gale began to blow, making the people fall over like ninepins and unable to dig the mountains.

顿时工地上狂风大作，人们东倒西歪，不能再挖山了。

Yet, Yu Gong told them to hold hands one after another to form a human wall, so the gale could no longer blow them down.

于是愚公让人们挽起手来，组成一道人墙，狂风就吹不倒他们了。

Then, Mountain God sent out a huge snake. The snake opened its bloody mouth and rushed at the people.

　　山神又放出一条巨蛇。巨蛇张着血盆大口，向人们扑了过来。

Yu Gong ordered them to jump aside, so the
huge snake failed to catch them.

愚公命令大家闪开，大蛇扑了个空。

Then, the people raised their hammers or shovels to hit the snake.

人们纷纷举起锤子、铁铲向大蛇打去。

After a fierce battle, the huge snake was beaten to death by the people.

一番大战之后，大蛇被人们打死了。

Mountain God had no way to defeat
them, so he ran up to the court of God
to report the matter to God.

山神无计可施，急忙跑到天
庭禀报了天帝。

God praised Yu Gong's persevering spirit greatly after hearing the story. Then, he sent two most mighty gods to help Yu Gong carry the two big mountains away.

天帝听后，对愚公的执著精神大加赞赏。于是，他派出两位力气最大的天神去帮助愚公搬走两座大山。

On the night of the same day, a god carried Mount Taihang to Suodong.

当天夜里，一位天神把太行山搬到了朔东。

Another god took Mount Wangwu to Yongnan.

另一位把王屋山搬到了雍南。

From then on, there was no longer any big mountain in the road, from the south of Jizhou to the north of Hanshui. People did farming here, living a peaceful and happy life.

　　从此，从冀州的南部，直到汉水的北部，再也没有大山挡路了。人们在这里种田耕作，过着安乐的生活。

Yu Gong's persevering and steadfast spirit has been remembered by the Chinese people from generation to generation.

愚公执著、坚定的精神被中华儿女世代称颂。

图书在版编目 （CIP）数据

愚公移山 / 蔡云晖等改编；蔡云晖等绘；刘光第译.
北京：海豚出版社，2005.10
（中国神话故事）
ISBN 7-80138-567-5

I. 愚... II. ①蔡... ②蔡... ③刘... III. 图画故
事—中国—当代—英汉 IV. I287.8

中国版本图书馆 CIP 数据核字（2005）第 115071 号

中国神话故事

愚公移山

改编：蔡云晖   张光帅
绘画：蔡云晖   张光帅
翻译：刘光第
社址：北京百万庄大街 24 号   邮编：100037
印刷：北京雷杰印刷有限公司
开本：16 开（787 毫米 × 1092 毫米）
文种：英汉   印张：3
版次：2005 年 10 月第 1 版 2006 年 2 月第 2 次印刷
标准书号：ISBN 7-80138-567-5
定价：15.00 元